Izzy
and the
Lost Butterfly

Written by

Lindsay Barlow & Lisa Becker

Illustrated by

Fuuji Takashi

Wisdom House Books

Dedication

To our parents, who have given and continue to give us unconditional love and support as we embark on this Adventure with Izzy.

To our families, who have listened to many drafts and revisions and kept us laughing. Especially our husbands who have supported us from the beginning.

To everyone at Wisdom House Books, who believed in us and gave us this chance to introduce Izzy to the world of readers.

To our Illustrator, Fuuji Takashi, who transformed our ideas into magical pictures.

And finally to each other . . . what a fun and exciting dream come true.

Meet Izzy!

Izzy is a curious eight-year-old girl.

She loves to learn new things, whether she is playing in her room or going on an adventure outside.

It's always exciting when she makes new friends along the way!

Read along to see where she will go and what she will find!

Izzy woke up
in the morning to the
sun shining bright.

WHOOPS!

She left her window
open all throughout
the night.

When Izzy went
to close it
something tiny
caught her eye.

It landed on her pillow.
It was a butterfly!

"You must be lost," she said to him.

"I know just what to do! You need some help to get back home.

Your family misses you!"

"Butterflies don't live inside,"
She exclaimed, as she drew near.

"Let's go outside to find your spot.
It's surely not in here."

Izzy held him in her hands
Until they reached the yard.

"Just give me clues along the way.
I know it won't be hard!"

"Now fly, fly, into the sky,
and show me where to go.

I'll watch the hints you
give me as you guide
me to your home."

First, he landed on a leaf,

Then dodged a rose's thorn.

Right on the petals he did sit,
next to roses being born.

He flew beside a honey bee
who buzzed around a hive;

The honey had a
sweet, sweet, smell,
and the bees all came alive.

He dove beneath a spider's web,
wet with morning dew.

On his way to a filled birdbath
where the birds were all wet, too!

He flew between some blades of grass
where mowing had been done.

And sat upon a sundial
that tells time with the sun.

"I know it's almost time to go,
I don't want this to end.

Let's take more adventures—
I'm glad you're my new friend!"

Then the butterfly crossed a picket fence—
The last and final clue.

Izzy climbed atop and took a peek;
His home came into view.

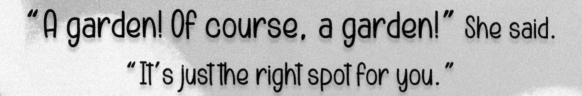

"A garden! Of course, a garden!" She said.
"It's just the right spot for you."

They smiled, waved, and said goodbye.
The butterfly fluttered, "Thank you."

Izzy found his home with help, of course.

She followed clues to find a beautiful,
colorful, perfect place,

For her new friend, the butterfly!

"Don't worry," she said to the butterfly.
"I'll be back to get you soon!

I can't wait
for our next adventure
while the garden is still in bloom."

The garden was full of colors,
so many to be told.

Their next adventure was coming
to find things bright and bold!

"Where should we go,
and what colors will we find next?"

Izzy and the Lost Butterfly

Published by Wisdom House Books, Inc.
Chapel Hill, North Carolina 27514 USA • 1.919.883.4669
www.wisdomhousebooks.com

Wisdom House Books is committed to excellence in the publishing industry.
Book design copyright © 2021 by Wisdom House Books, Inc.
All rights reserved.

Cover and Interior Illustration by Fuuji Takashi
Cover and Interior design by Ted Ruybal
Published in the United States of America
Hardback ISBN: 978-1-7356291-0-0
LCCN: 2021903044

JUV002300 | JUVENILE FICTION / Animals / Butterflies, Moths & Caterpillars
JUV020000 | JUVENILE FICTION / Interactive Adventures
JUV039060 | JUVENILE FICTION / Social Themes / Friendship

First Edition

25 24 23 22 21 20 / 10 9 8 7 6 5 4 3 2 1

Lisa Becker is a writer, author and community volunteer located in Chapel Hill, NC. She earned a M.Ed. in curriculum and instruction from Doane College in 2000 and a B.S. in Elementary and Early Childhood Education from Northwest Missouri State University in 1998. She taught second grade for more than a decade in three different states including inner city school districts and served many more as a substitute teacher. In addition to her extensive volunteer service at Open M in Akron OH, she was an active track and cross-country coach for elementary and middle school children. She started writing children's books with her sister, Lindsay Barlow, to stay in touch, to find an outlet for her creativity and to continue her passion for instilling the love of reading in elementary age children. In her free time she enjoys exercise, travel and watching her children participate in sports and dance.

About the Authors

Lindsay Barlow is an elementary school Art Instructor in Highlands Ranch, Colorado. In addition to teaching, she is a family photographer and author. She worked in the media for 20 years after graduating from the University of Iowa with a degree in Film, Television and Radio Production. She worked in film and television both in the United States and Internationally for CNN, CNN International, NBC Universal and STARZ Entertainment. While living abroad in Europe and New Zealand, she started seriously pursuing her writing and partnered with her sister, Lisa Becker, to fulfill her dream of writing children's books. She loves living near the mountains with her family and skiing whenever she can.

About the Illustrator

Fuuji Takashi is a children's book illustrator and character designer. She is most notable for her works on children's books featuring diverse characters. For her works on kid's literature, her artworks have been featured in both local and international news. Her illustrations have been published in both digital media and prints around the world.

Fuuji's love for art justified her shift of career from a professional nurse to an artist. While she considers nursing a noble job, nothing fulfills her more than being able to create and bring joy to people through her art. Her greatest creative influences are Ghibli and Disney films. In her spare time, she likes singing, cooking, and taking long peaceful walks.

CPSIA information can be obtained
at www.ICGtesting.com
Printed in the USA
BVHW021220190821
614777BV00006B/520

9 781735 629100